STOP THIEF!

by
Adam
J. B. Lane

A NEAL PORTER BOOK

ROARING BROOK PRESS

NEW YORK

For Rebecca,
the
perfect
partner-in-crime

Copyright © 2012 by Adam J. B. Lane

A Neal Porter Book

Published by Roaring Brook Press

Roaring Brook Press is a division of Holtzbrinck Publishing Holdings Limited Partnership

175 Fifth Avenue, New York, New York 10010

mackids.com

Library of Congress Cataloging-in-Publication Data

Lane, Adam.

  Stop thief! / Adam J.B. Lane. — 1st ed.

    p. cm.

  "A Neal Porter Book."

  Summary: Randall McCoy declares to his parents that he is a big boy and
no longer needs his stuffed pig, but creeps downstairs later and finds a
robber taking Mr. Pigglesworth, which sets off a wild chase through the
night to stop the thief.

  ISBN 978-1-59643-693-0

  [1. Adventure and adventurers—Fiction. 2. Robbers and outlaws—Fiction.
3. Growth—Fiction.] I. Title.

  PZ7.L2317577Sto 2012

  [E]—dc23

                        2011013505

Roaring Brook Press books are available for special promotions and premiums.
For details contact: Director of Special Markets, Holtzbrinck Publishers.

First edition 2012

Printed in China by Macmillan Production (Asia) Ltd., Kwun Tong, Kowloon, Hong Kong (supplier code 10)

10 9 8 7 6 5 4 3 2 1

One evening after dinner, Randall McCoy stood up on his chair and announced as loud as he could:

This was news to his mother and father.

Randall's dad thought for a minute.

"Well," he said, "I'm sure you still need Mr. Pigglesworth. You can't be too old for him."

"No, I am," Randall answered. And he put his stuffed pig up on the shelf and marched straight upstairs to bed.

BUT . . .

Alone in the quiet of his room, Randall could not sleep.

He tried different positions:

TUCKED

UN-TUCKED

OVER THE COVERS

UNDER THE BED

WRONG WAY ROUND

Nothing worked. Perhaps he needed Mr. Pigglesworth after all.

Randall climbed out of bed and crept silently down the stairs. But when he turned on the light . . .

he saw a strange man stealing his pig!

he cried. But the robber ran away instead.

So Randall chased after him—out of the house and into the star-flecked night.

The
Vegetables

The Factor

The Key
To The City

Strange constellations danced and spun overhead.

The Bumper Car

The Elephant

The Balloon

The Booster Seat

The Skyscraper

The Airplane

The Chocolate Bar

And as they ran all around town, Randall shouted

Only this last time, instead of running, the crook hopped into a hot air balloon and soared off into the sky.

BALLOON RIDES 25¢

There was no time to think. Randall grabbed for the rope and . . .

A steady breeze carried the balloon high over   the city.

Randall could see for miles all around.

The wind
shifted and the
balloon began
to sink. A huge
skyscraper rose
up to meet it.

But the robber was too busy looking at Randall to see where they were heading. So what did Randall yell?

Too late!
SMASH!
CRASH!
The balloon got snagged on the edge of the building.
The criminal was left hanging on for dear life!

It was Randall to the rescue!

And then they were
pulled to safety.

Nobody the thief had robbed had ever saved his life before.
The more he thought about it, the worse he felt.

Fortunately, giving Randall his pig back
cheered him up a little.

Everyone made a big fuss over the boy hero. The mayor was ready to give Randall the key to the city!

But by now it was very, very late, and Randall just wanted to go home to bed.

A motorcade with sirens blaring drove to Randall's house. "What's going on?" yawned Mom and Dad.

The mayor explained what a grown-up boy Randall was . . .

but he was already fast asleep.

The mayor and her motorcade headed back to town as quietly as they could.

Meanwhile, Randall's parents carried him to his room. They tucked him in and kissed him good night, with Mr. Pigglesworth right beside him.

And even though he was certainly a big boy now,

that was just what he wanted.